THE KINGFISHER TREASURY OF

Five-Minute Stories

For Lily and Toby,
with much love – F. W.

For Tom, Toby
and Annie – J. L.

KINGFISHER
An imprint of Kingfisher Publications Plc
New Penderel House, 283-288 High Holborn
London WC1V 7HZ
www.kingfisherpub.com

First published by Kingfisher 2000
This edition published by Kingfisher 2005
4 6 8 10 9 7 5 3

A CIP catalogue record for this book is available from the British Library.

ISBN-13: 978 0 7534 1156 8

Printed in India
3TR/0107/THOM/FR(MA)/70STORA

THE KINGFISHER TREASURY OF

Five-Minute Stories

CHOSEN BY FIONA WATERS

ILLUSTRATED BY JOHN LAWRENCE

KINGFISHER

CONTENTS

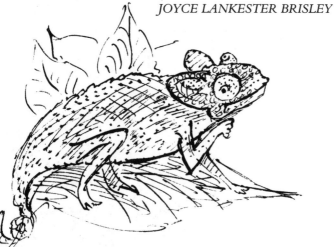

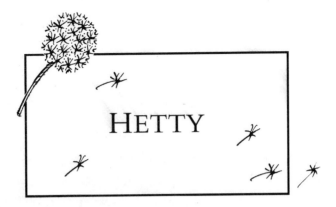

HETTY

Anne Fine

Once upon a time there was a plain little grey worm called Hetty who wanted, more than anything in the world, to be a glow-worm.

"Don't be silly," said her father. "Glow-worms are *different*."

"It's no use even thinking about it," said her mother.

But Hetty couldn't help thinking about it. She thought about it all the time. She imagined having a glow inside her, a glow she could turn on and off like an electric light.

She could light the way home through the woods when it was dark . . .

She could find things people had lost in murky corners . . .

Best of all, she could read secretly in bed at night, without anyone catching her.

She longed to be a glow-worm.

"Never mind," said her mother. "Come and have a cuddle."

"Never mind," said her father. "Have a gingerbread star."

But Hetty wasn't satisfied with cuddles and gingerbread stars. She wanted to be a glow-worm, and she'd be one, whatever they said. So she went out in the garden and sat on a flowerpot, thinking.

And when she had finished, she slipped off her flowerpot and made her way quietly out of the garden, all the way through the woods till she reached the royal castle.

The queen was busy counting all her coins. "What you are looking for is magic," she said. "I only have money and power. Go and ask the wizard."

Hetty found the wizard at the top of the highest tower. He was busy petting and soothing his assistant. A spell had gone wrong, and all her paws had turned bright pink and purple. She was worse than upset. She was sulking. She wouldn't even go and fetch the spell book so he could turn her paws back to jet black again.

"You hold the wand," the wizard said to Hetty. "I'll fetch the spell book." And off he went, the cat tucked under his arm.

Hetty was left all alone. She was left all alone for a very long time. She was cold. She was bored. And she was very, very hungry.

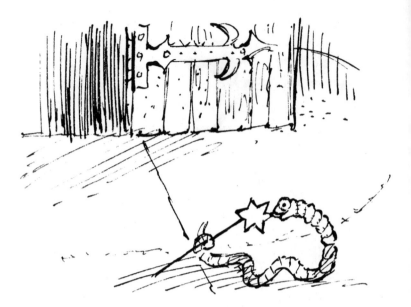

She looked at the star at the end of the wizard's magic wand. It was golden and glowing, like freshly baked gingerbread. She sniffed. It smelt like gingerbread. She pressed. It felt like gingerbread. She licked. It tasted like gingerbread.

And she was very, very hungry indeed.

All of a sudden, before she even realized what she was doing, Hetty had gobbled up the star, whole, all in one go.

She was horrified. And she could hear the wizard coming back!

Now Hetty was foolish, and she was stubborn too. But she was not stupid. She knew, whenever you swallow something funny, you have to tell, and straightaway.

"Excuse me," she said to the wizard politely. "I have just gobbled up the star at the end of your wand, by mistake."

But the wizard did not hear her. He was too busy looking for the star at the end of his wand.

"Please," said Hetty again. "I have eaten the star off the end of your wand."

"Just a moment," said the wizard impatiently. "I cannot solve anybody's problems until I have found the star at the end of my wand."

Hetty burst into tears.

The cat stopped sulking to explain the problem to the wizard.

The wizard took it very well, considering. "Thank you for telling me," he said to Hetty.

"It's always best to tell," agreed the cat. "And there are plenty more wand stars in the cupboard. We bake them twice a week, and put the magic filling in on Thursdays."

"So," Hetty said, "I am not poisoned?"

"Poisoned?" exclaimed the wizard. "Certainly not! What a rude suggestion! The worst that will happen to you is that you'll start to glow a bit, inside."

"Like a glow-worm?" asked Hetty, getting excited. "Like a *glow-worm*?"

"I'm afraid so," said the wizard.

"How long will it last?" asked Hetty.

"Till you grow up," said the wizard. "If you are frugal, and do not leave it on all night."

"Oh, bliss!" breathed Hetty. "Oh, joy!"

"We'd better take her home," observed the cat. "It's getting dark."

They all set off together. The cat wore boots.

On the way home, Hetty kept glowing in the gathering dusk. It was a bit embarrassing. She tried to distract the cat and the wizard by pointing out bits of the scenery . . .

. . . until she got the knack of switching on and off.

Just as they arrived at the garden gate, Hetty's father came out and called her in for supper.

"Goodbye," said the wizard. "It was nice to meet you, even though I never did find out what it was you wanted."

"I don't want anything," said Hetty. "I have everything I want."

And so she did. She lit the way home through the woods when it was dark . . .

She found things people had lost in murky corners . . .

And, best of all, she could read secretly in bed at night without anyone catching her.

And, since she was careful and never left it on all night, it lasted till she was grown up.

THE STRANGE EGG

Margaret Mahy

Once Molly found a strange leathery egg in the swamp. She put it under Mrs Warm the broody hen to hatch it out. It hatched out into a sort of dragon.

Her father said, "This is no ordinary dragon. This is a dinosaur."

"What is a dinosaur?" asked Molly.

"Well," said her father, "a long time ago there were a lot of dinosaurs. They were all big lizards. Some of them were bigger than houses. They all died a long time ago . . . All except this one," he added gloomily. "I hope it is not one of the larger meat-eating lizards as then it might grow up to worry sheep."

The dinosaur followed Mrs Warm about. She scratched worms for it, but the dinosaur liked plants better.

16

"Ah," said Molly's father. "It is a plant-eating dinosaur — one of the milder kind. They are stupid but good-natured," he added.

Professors of all ages came from near and far to see Molly's dinosaur. She led it around on a string. Every day she needed a longer piece of string. The dinosaur grew as big as ten elephants. It ate all the flowers in the garden and Molly's mother got cross.

"I am tired of having no garden and I am tired of making tea for all the professors," she said. "Let's send the dinosaur to the zoo."

"No," said Father. "The place wouldn't be the same without it."

So the dinosaur stayed. Mrs Warm used to perch on it every night. She had never before hatched such a grand and successful egg.

One day it began to rain . . . It rained and rained and rained and rained and rained so heavily that the water in the river got deep and overflowed.

"A flood, a flood – we will drown," screamed Molly's mother.

"Hush, dear," said Molly's father. "We will ride to a safe place on Molly's dinosaur. Whistle to him, Molly."

Molly whistled and the dinosaur came towards her with Mrs Warm the hen, wet and miserable, on his back. Molly and her father and mother climbed on to the dinosaur's back with her. They held an umbrella over themselves and had warm drinks out of a thermos flask. Just as they left, the house was swept away by the flood.

"Well, dear, there you are," said Molly's father. "You see it was useful to have a dinosaur, after all. And I am now able to tell you that this is the biggest kind of dinosaur and its name is Brontosaurus."

Molly was pleased to think her pet had such a long, dignified-sounding name. It matched him well. As they went along they rescued a lot of other people climbing trees and house tops, and floating on chicken crates and fruit boxes. They rescued cats and dogs, two horses and an elephant which was floating away from a circus. The dinosaur paddled on cheerfully. By the time they came in sight of dry land, his back was quite crowded. On the land policemen were getting boats ready to go looking for people, but all the people were safe on the dinosaur's back.

After the flood went down and everything was as it should be, a fine medal was given to Molly's dinosaur as most heroic animal of the year and many presents were given to him.

The biggest present of all was a great big swimming pool made of rubber so you could blow it up. It was so big it took one man nearly a year to blow it up. It was a good size for dinosaurs of the Brontosaurus type. He lived in the swimming pool after that (and Molly's mother was able to grow her flowers again). It is well known that Brontosauruses like to swim and paddle. It took the weight off his feet. Mrs Warm the hen used to swim with him a bit, and it is not very often that you find a swimming hen.

So you see this story has a happy ending after all, which is not easy with a pet as big as ten elephants. And just to end the story I must tell you that though Molly's dinosaur had the long name of Brontosaurus, Molly always called it "Rosie".

THE TOWN MOUSE AND THE COUNTRY MOUSE

Aesop
Retold by Fiona Waters

There was once a gentle mouse who lived quietly in the country. His larder was always full and in the winter he was snug and cosy in his little house with his comfy bed lined with wool from his neighbour the sheep. He was well contented with his simple way of life.

One day, when the sun was shining and the birds were singing, he decided to invite his friend the Town Mouse to stay for a few days. He rushed round collecting the best nuts and berries he could find and then went to meet his friend at the crossroads.

Now the Town Mouse was rather inclined to look down on his friend and I am very sorry to say he wrinkled his haughty nose when he saw the nuts and berries. He ate only the finest cheese and

chocolate and rich cream cakes. The straw was scratchy and prickly under his delicate paws, which were used to soft carpets.

The next morning, the Country Mouse had been out and about since sunrise when the Town Mouse eventually appeared, yawning and scratching himself.

"I do hope you slept well," said the Country Mouse, who had given up his own bed for his visitor.

"Oh dear me, no," said the ungracious Town Mouse. "I have tossed and turned *all* night without a *wink* of sleep and the sheep's wool made me sneeze. Then the birds started making the most dreadful noise before it was even light."

The poor Country Mouse was most upset that his friend had not been comfortable, but he bustled round preparing a huge breakfast of fresh field mushrooms and barley. The Town Mouse merely picked at his food and looked decidedly bored.

"What are we going to do today to amuse ourselves?" he asked. "What parties are we going to?"

"I don't really go to parties," said the Country Mouse.

"It all sounds very *dull*," said the Town Mouse severely. "My dear fellow, you must come up to town with me immediately and I will show you what a fine time I have." And he swept out of the door and was off down the road before the Country Mouse had time to draw his breath.

When they arrived in the town the poor Country Mouse was absolutely terrified by all the noise and dirt and smells and the people rushing

about. He was very relieved when his friend dived down some steep stairs and they emerged into an enormous room.

"My, oh my," said the Country Mouse, staring with complete bewilderment at the magnificence before him.

Candlelight flickered off glowing silver plates and sparkling glasses, and the vast table was covered in plates of the most delicious food he had ever imagined. There were great rounds of cheese, huge joints of meat, platters piled with fruits and nuts, and jellies and cakes and big bowls of cream. The Country Mouse was quite speechless at such opulence.

"I had no idea you lived in such splendour. Thank you, my friend, for sharing it all with me. Just look at this cheese! It is as big as a wagon wheel, and what a great heap of red apples. There are more here than in my entire orchard!" said the awe-struck Country Mouse.

And then a truly *dreadful* thing happened. Just as the Country Mouse drew a deep breath to exclaim again at the splendour of the feast, there came the most frightening snarl and there, with its big paws on the edge of the table, stood a huge and very cross cat. The Country Mouse gave one terrified squeak, dived off the table, scrabbled his way along the skirting board until he came to a gap and squeezed in with a great gasp. He was only just in time. He tried to make himself as small as possible as the cat peered in the hole with one great fierce eye. And so they sat for what seemed ages, until eventually the cat became bored and slunk off. The poor Country Mouse collapsed in a heap, sobbing.

And then he heard a yawn and, "Ah, there you are, my dear fellow! I'm so sorry, I quite forgot to mention the stupid cat. But the coast is clear. We can go back now."

"Go back!" exclaimed the Country Mouse. "I wouldn't *dream* of going back. You may have very fine food, but I'm afraid I couldn't enjoy eating in such alarming company. I'm off home to my dull life in the country, where at least I can eat my

simple nuts and berries in safety." And he scuttled off as fast as ever he could go. He didn't stop running until he reached his own wee house and his own comfy bed.

And only then did he realize that he hadn't even tasted one single mouthful of all that delicious food!

THE GLASS CUPBOARD

Terry Jones

There was once a cupboard that was made entirely of glass so you could see right into it and right through it. Now, although this cupboard always appeared to be empty, you could always take out whatever you wanted. If you wanted a cool drink, for example, you just opened the cupboard and took one out. Or if you wanted a new pair of shoes, you could always take a pair out of the glass cupboard. Even if you wanted a bag of gold, you just opened up the glass cupboard and took out a bag of gold. The only thing you had to remember was that, whenever you took something *out* of the glass cupboard, you had to put something else back *in*, although nobody quite knew why.

Naturally such a valuable thing as the glass cupboard belonged to a rich and powerful King.

One day, the King had to go on a long journey,

and while he was gone some thieves broke into the palace and stole the glass cupboard.

"Now we can have anything we want," they said.

One of the robbers said: "I want a large bag of gold," and he opened the glass cupboard and took out a large bag of gold.

Then the second robber said: "I want two large bags of gold," and he opened the glass cupboard and took out two large bags of gold.

Then the chief of the robbers said: "I want three of the biggest bags of gold you've ever seen!" and he opened the glass cupboard and took out three of the biggest bags of gold you've ever seen.

"Hooray!" they said. "Now we can take out as much gold as we like!"

Well, those three robbers stayed up the whole night, taking bag after bag of gold out of the glass cupboard. But not one of them put anything back in.

In the morning, the chief of the robbers said: "Soon we shall be the richest three men in the world. But let us go to sleep now, and we can take out more gold tonight."

So they lay down to sleep. But the first robber could not sleep. He kept thinking: "If I went to the glass cupboard just *once* more, I'd be even richer than I am now." So he got up, and went to the cupboard, and took out yet another bag of gold, and then went back to bed.

And the second robber could not sleep either. He kept thinking: "If I went to the glass cupboard and took out two more bags of gold, I'd be even richer than the others." So he got up, and went to the cupboard, and took out two more bags of gold, and then went back to bed.

Meanwhile the chief of the robbers could not sleep either. He kept thinking: "If I went to the glass cupboard and took out three more bags of gold, I'd be the richest of all." So he got up, and went to the cupboard, and took out three more bags of gold, and then went back to bed.

And then the first robber said to himself: "What am I doing, lying here sleeping, when I could be getting richer?" So he got up, and started taking more and more bags of gold out of the cupboard.

The second robber heard him and thought: "What am I doing, lying here sleeping, when he's getting richer than me?" So he got up and joined his companion.

And then the chief of the robbers got up too. "I can't lie here sleeping," he said, "while the other two are both getting richer than me." So he got up and soon all three were hard at it, taking more and more bags of gold out of the cupboard.

And all that day and all that night not one of them dared to stop for fear that one of his companions would get richer than him. And they carried on all the next day and all the next night. They didn't stop to rest, and they didn't stop to eat, and they didn't even stop to drink. They kept taking out those bags of gold faster and faster and more and more until, at length,

they grew faint with lack of sleep and food and drink, but still they did not dare to stop.

All that week and all the next week, and all that month and all that winter, they kept at it, until the chief of the robbers could bear it no longer, and he picked up a hammer and smashed the glass cupboard into a million pieces, and they all three gave a great cry and fell down dead on top of the huge mountain of gold they had taken out of the glass cupboard.

Some time later the King returned home, and his servants threw themselves on their knees before him, and said: "Forgive us, Your Majesty, but three wicked robbers have stolen the glass cupboard!"

The King ordered his servants to search the length and breadth of the land. When they found what was left of the glass cupboard, and the three robbers lying dead, they filled sixty great carts with all the gold and took it back to the King. And when the King heard that the glass cupboard was smashed into a million pieces and that the three thieves were dead, he shook his head and said: "If those thieves had always put something back into the cupboard for every bag of gold they had taken out, they would be alive to this day." And he ordered his servants to collect all the pieces of the glass cupboard and to melt them down and make them into a globe with all the countries of the world upon it, to remind himself, and others, that the earth is as fragile as that glass cupboard.

A BLIND MAN CATCHES A BIRD

An African folk tale
retold by Alexander McCall Smith

A young man married a woman whose brother was blind. The young man was eager to get to know his new brother-in-law and so he asked him if he would like to go hunting with him.

"I cannot see," the blind man said. "But you can help me see when we are out hunting together. We can go."

The young man led the blind man off into the bush. At first they followed a path that he knew and it was easy for the blind man to tag on behind the other. After a while, though, they went off into thicker bush, where the trees grew closely together and there were many places for the animals to hide. The blind man now held on to the arm of his sighted brother-in-law and told him many things about the sounds that they heard around them.

Because he had no sight, he had a great ability to interpret the noises made by animals in the bush.

"There are warthogs around," he would say. "I can hear their noises over there."

Or: "That bird is preparing to fly. Listen to the sound of its wings unfolding."

To the brother-in-law, these sounds were meaningless, and he was most impressed at the blind man's ability to understand the bush although it must have been for him one great darkness.

They walked on for several hours, until they reached a place where they could set their traps. The blind man followed the other's advice, and put his trap in a place where birds might come for water. The other man put his trap a short distance away, taking care to disguise it so that no bird would know that it was there. He did not bother to disguise the blind man's trap, as it was hot and he was eager to get home to his new wife. The blind man thought that he had disguised his trap, but he did not see that he had failed to do so and any bird could tell that there was a trap there.

They returned to their hunting place the next day. The blind man was excited at the prospect of having caught something, and the young man had to tell him to keep quiet, or he would scare all the animals away. Even before they reached the traps, the blind man was able to tell that they had caught something.

"I can hear the birds," he said. "There are birds in the traps."

When he reached his trap, the young man saw that he had caught a small bird. He took it out of the trap and put it in a pouch that he had brought with him. Then the two of them walked towards the blind man's trap.

"There is a bird in it," he said to the blind man. "You have caught a bird too."

As he spoke, he felt himself filling with jealousy.

The blind man's bird was marvellously coloured, as if it had flown through a rainbow and been stained by the colours. The feathers from a bird such as that would make a fine present for his new wife, but the blind man had a wife too, and she would also want the feathers.

The young man bent down and took the blind man's bird from the trap. Then, quickly substituting his own bird, he passed it to the blind man and put the coloured bird into his own pouch.

"Here is your bird," he said to the blind man. "You may put it in your pouch."

The blind man reached
out for the bird and took it. He felt
it for a moment, his fingers passing
over the wings and the breast. Then,
without saying anything, he put the
bird into his pouch and they began
the trip home.

On their way home, the two men
stopped to rest under a broad tree. As
they sat there, they talked about many
things. The young man was impressed
with the wisdom of the blind man,
who knew a great deal, although he
could see nothing at all.

"Why do people fight
with one another?" he
asked the blind man. It
was a question which
had always troubled
him and he
wondered if the
blind man could
give him an
answer.

The blind man said nothing for a few moments, but it was clear to the young man that he was thinking. Then the blind man raised his head, and it seemed to the young man as if the unseeing eyes were staring right into his soul. Quietly he gave his answer.

"Men fight because they do to each other what you have just done to me."

The words shocked the young man and made him ashamed. He tried to think of a response, but none came. Rising to his feet, he fetched his pouch, took out the brightly coloured bird and gave it back to the blind man.

The blind man took the bird, felt over it with his fingers, and smiled.

"Do you have any other questions for me?" he asked.

"Yes," said the young man. "How do men become friends after they have fought?"

The blind man smiled again.

"They do what you have just done," he said. "That's how they become friends again."

THE BEAR WHO LIKED HUGGING PEOPLE

Ruth Ainsworth

There was once a bear who lived in a cave in the mountains. He was a mountain bear. He ate fruit and berries and did no harm to anybody, but he had one bad habit. He *would* hug people. He only hugged them because he liked them, but they did not know that. His furry arms were so strong that he hugged much too tightly. Some of the people he hugged were never the same again. They were quite flat when he let them go, and lopsided.

Not many people went along the rough track that passed the door of his cave, but he never failed to rush at them, his arms outstretched, to give them a loving hug.

The people living near dared not pass that way or let their children go by alone. They used, instead, a very long, steep, rocky path that led them

right up on the side of the mountain. It took much longer and was difficult to find at night or in the snow.

The mothers were particularly worried about their children who emerged from the bear's hug quite a different shape, flat instead of round, with snub noses which completely changed their expression.

The men of the neighbourhood met together to decide what to do for the best. Should they catch the bear and put him in a cage in a zoo? Or should they shoot him and make something useful out of his fur, a coat or a rug? They decided, rather sadly, to shoot him, and the wife of the man who shot him should be given the skin for a fur coat. They were upset about this, but there seemed no other way out. They could not risk their little children being deformed and it did not seem as though the bear would change his habits.

About this time, a poor man who lived far away, on the other side of the mountain, decided to go and visit his old mother who lived down in the valley. He had saved downy goose feathers to make a deep, billowy feather bed to give her as a present. One day, he left home and travelled over the mountain with the new feather bed rolled up and strapped on his back.

When he got near the cave where the bear lived, the bear smelled him coming and came lumbering out into the sunshine, his furry arms outstretched. The traveller remembered hearing stories of a bear who hugged people and he called out loudly: "Lord Bear. I've brought you a present. I've brought you something warm and just made to be hugged. Wait while I unstrap it from my back."

The bear waited, because he was a good-natured fellow, and when the bed was unstrapped, but still in a roll, he took it in his arms and gave it a tight, close hug.

It did not struggle or cry out. It melted into his arms with softness and warmth.

"Keep it," said the traveller, shaking with fear. "Keep it, my Lord. I made it for you."

This was not really true as he had made it for his old mother, but a man may change his mind. And the bear did not know about the old mother.

So he kept it and carried it into his cave and hugged it every night, when he went to sleep. This satisfied him and he quite gave up hugging other people. The men in the neighbourhood gave up the horrid idea of shooting him, too. Even the smallest children were now quite safe when passing his cave door alone.

All the cold, dark winter the bear dozed in his cave, under the snow, his feather bed held tightly in his arms.

When the spring came with flowers and birds, he woke up and was lucky enough to meet with a wife, a young bear just old enough to get married. So if he felt like hugging anybody, she was always near at hand and loved to be hugged.

As for the feather bed, they kept it in the cave and slept on it. This was much more comfortable than lying on the hard, rocky floor.

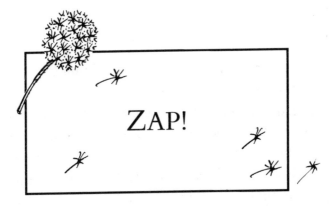

ZAP!

Dick King-Smith

Of all the chameleons in Africa, Kenneth was the most unhappy. He couldn't change colour.

Kenneth could do all the other things that chameleons do.

He could walk along a thin branch, holding it with two fingers of each hand.

He could roll his eyes in different directions at the same time.

He could shoot out his long sticky tongue and, sometimes, zap a fly.

But his brothers and his sisters and his friends could do the cleverest thing of all.

They could change the colour of their skins.

If they sat on a greenish leaf, they turned greenish.

If they sat on a reddish flower, they turned reddish.

If they sat on yellowish sand, they turned yellowish.

But Kenneth always stayed the same colour – a sort of muddy brown.

However hard he tried, he didn't seem to be able to get the hang of changing. He was always muddy brown.

So he could only zap flies when he sat on brown mud.

So he didn't zap many flies.

He was the most unhappy chameleon in Africa.

One day Kenneth was sitting on a leaf, trying to zap flies. The leaf was silvery, so the flies could see him easily; and one after another they buzzed off laughing.

"Oh dear!" said Kenneth, rolling his tongue back up, after the fifteenth miss.

"What's the trouble?" said a voice, and Kenneth looked round.

There on the next branch was a pretty young female chameleon whose name was Kiki.

Kenneth sighed.

"I'm feeling blue," he said.

"You don't look it," said Kiki. "Why do you stay muddy brown on a silvery leaf?"

Kenneth was ashamed. He rolled his eyes in different directions.

"I can't change," he said. "All my brothers and sisters and friends can change colour, but I can't get the hang of it. I wish I could. I'm green with envy."

"You don't look it," said Kiki again. "But," she said softly, "I'll tell you what you do look."

"What?"

"You look very handsome."

Kenneth felt terribly embarrassed.

"There!" she cried. "You can do it!"

Kenneth kept one eye on Kiki, and rolled the other one backwards to look at himself. He had turned bright red!

"You see," said Kiki, "you felt embarrassed, didn't you?"

"Yes," said Kenneth.

"Well, there you are. If you want to be green, for instance, try *feeling* envious."

So he tried, and sure enough, he turned green.

Then Kiki told him to pretend feeling frightened, and he turned yellow; and to feel angry, and he turned black; and to feel old and tired, and he turned grey.

"Now," said Kiki, "try feeling unhappy."

"No," said Kenneth, rolling his eyes madly. "Now I've met you, blue's the one colour I'm never going to be. Let's go fly-zapping!"

And from then on, the flies never had another chance to laugh at Kenneth the chameleon.

Zap! they never knew what hit them.

THE MAN WHO DIDN'T WASH HIS DISHES

Phyllis Krasilovsky

There once was a man who lived alone in a little house on the edge of a town. He didn't have a wife or children, so he always cooked his own supper, cleaned the house by himself, and made his own bed.

One night he came home hungrier than usual, so he made himself a big, big supper. It was a very good supper (he liked to cook and could make good things to eat), but there was so much of it that he grew very, very tired by the time he'd finished. He just sat back in his chair, as full as he could be, and decided he'd leave the dishes till the next night, and then he would wash them all at once.

But the next night he was *twice* as hungry, so he cooked twice as big a supper, and took twice as long to eat it, and was twice as tired by the time he'd finished. So he left those dishes in the sink, too.

Well, as the days went by he got hungrier and hungrier, and more and more tired, and so he never washed his dishes. After a while there were so many dirty dishes that they didn't all fit in the sink. So he began to pile them on the table.

Soon the table was so full that he began to put them on his bookshelves. And when *they* were full, he put them just everywhere he could find

an empty place. Soon he had them all piled on the floor, too. In fact, the floor got to be so full of dishes that he had a hard time getting into his house at night – they were even piled against the door!

Then one night he looked in his closet and found that there wasn't one clean dish left! He was hungry enough to eat out of anything, so he ate out of the soap dish from the bathroom.

It was too dirty for him to use again the next night, so he used one of his ashtrays.

Pretty soon he had used up all his ashtrays.

Then he ate out of some clean flowerpots he found down the cellar. When *they* were all used up, he ate out of his candy dishes and drank water from vases.

He used up *everything* finally – even the pots he cooked his food in, and he didn't know what to do! He was *soooo* unhappy. His whole house was full of dirty dishes – and dirty flowerpots – and dirty ashtrays – and dirty candy dishes – and dirty pots – and a dirty soap dish. He couldn't even find his books – or his alarm clock – or even his bed any more! He couldn't sit down to think because even his chairs were filled with dishes, and he couldn't find the sink so he could wash them!

But then – all of a sudden – it began to rain! And the man got an idea. He drove his big truck around to the side of the house and piled up all the dishes – and all the vases – and all the flowerpots – and all the ashtrays – and all the candy dishes – and the soap dish – on it, and drove the truck out into the rain.

The rain fell on everything and soon they were clean again. THE RAIN HAD WASHED THEM!

Then the man carried everything back into the house again. He put the dishes in the dish closet, the pots in the pot closet, the ashtrays on the tables, the candy dishes on the shelves, the flowerpots in

the cellar, the vases where the vases go, and the soap dish in the bathroom. He was so very, very tired after carrying everything back and putting it away that he decided that from then on he would always wash his dishes just as soon as he had finished his supper.

The next night when he came home he cooked his supper, and – when he had finished eating it – he washed the dishes and put them right away. He did this every night after that, too. He is very happy now. He can find his chairs, and he can find his alarm clock, and he can find his bed. It is easy for him to get into his house, too, because there are no more dishes piled on the floor – or anywhere!

THE WOMAN WHO GREW BUTTERFLIES

Wendy Eyton

In the little town of Bunting stood a neat row of cottages. The cottage steps were always freshly washed, and the doors were brightly painted in all the colours of the rainbow.

"There never was a row as pretty as ours," said Mrs Gordon, who lived in the first cottage.

"And our gardens are a sight for sore eyes," said Mr Bennett, who lived in the second cottage.

"All except for one," sighed Mr and Mrs Bunce, who lived in the third cottage. "And that's not a sight for sore eyes, it's nothing but an eyesore."

And they pointed to the fourth cottage, where Old Molly lived.

Old Molly, you see, was very kind to animals. And not just animals, either. She fed the birds with bread and nuts and grain in the winter months. And in the summer she would not tread on a snail or slug if she could help it.

Her neighbours would not allow snails and slugs in their gardens. And more than anything they hated caterpillars. They went to the gardening shop and bought spray guns and puffer bottles which kill at the touch of a button. So all the snails and slugs and caterpillars made their way to Old Molly's garden. She had not the heart to harm them, and soon they had eaten everything in sight!

"That silly woman hasn't a single flower left," sniffed Mrs Gordon, as she tended her roses.

"And look at her apple tree. Not a leaf on it," sneered Mr Bennett, as he trimmed his hedge.

"She won't stand a chance in the competition," sniggered Mr and Mrs Bunce.

"What the Mayor will say we can't imagine."

For in a week's time the Mayor of Bunting was to choose the most beautiful garden and present the owner with a big silver cup.

"I will fill it with roses from my garden," thought Mrs Gordon, as she polished her sideboard.

"I will put it in the window, where everyone can see it," thought Mr Bennett, as he trimmed his hedge another few inches.

"I will have it on my side of the bed one week," said Mr Bunce.

"And I will have it on my side the other," agreed his wife.

Old Molly was not thinking of roses or

hedgerows or silver cups. She was looking at the caterpillars in her garden, which had grown so fat they had stopped eating and wrapped themselves up in bundles.

"You'll soon be bursting out of your skins," she chuckled. "And then what little beauties you will be."

Seven days later the Mayor of Bunting arrived. He drove the car himself, and the bonnet of his car was painted to look like a large bumblebee. His waistcoat was embroidered with bluebottles, and from his ear dangled an earring shaped like a golden ant.

First he looked at Mrs Gordon's garden, at her lawn as neat as a pocket-handkerchief, her spiky trellis-work and roses.

"Ten marks out of fifty for trying," said the Mayor.

Then he looked at Mr Bennett's garden, his well-trimmed hedge, his well-tended patio and his garden gnomes.

"Five out of fifty," said the Mayor, who did not like garden gnomes.

He was about to give Mr and Mrs Bunce eight points each for their lily pond when his eye was attracted to Old Molly's garden.

For in the night the butterflies had climbed out of their hard little caterpillar-jackets and they were clinging to all the branches of the apple tree. They quivered and gleamed in the sunlight like thousands of blossoms – orange, flame-red, lavender and mauve.

The slugs and snails had been busy in the night, too, and the yard outside Old Molly's house was patterned in shining silver. On the roof white fluffy doves, rosy finches and tiny bluetits preened themselves and twittered and cooed.

"What a magnificent sight!" cried the Mayor, rubbing the bluebottles on his waistcoat.

"Two hundred out of fifty, without any doubt."

Then he gave Old Molly the big silver cup and drove home, humming an opera tune, for egg on toast, honey sandwiches and rose-hip tea.

Old Molly stared at the cup. She saw the reflection of her wizened brown face and giggled.

Then she put the cup on her mantelpiece and it stayed there for the rest of the summer, and throughout the winter, too.

But with the coming of spring, Old Molly was too busy to clean silver. So she put the cup in the garden, and a robin built her nest in it.

THE SOUP-STONE

Leila Berg

Now this is the tale of a very odd stone. And this is the way I tell it.

Once upon a time there was a man, and he was very poor. He had no money to buy any food, and so of course he was very hungry. Well, he was walking along, wondering what he could do to get some dinner, when he bent down and picked up a stone from the roadway – yes, a big stone.

Then he knocked at someone's door. A woman answered it.

"Good morning," said the man.

"Good morning. What's that you have there?"

"Oh, that's my soup-stone."

"Whatever is a soup-stone?"

"It's a stone for making soup, of course."

"A stone for making soup! I've never heard of

such a thing. Are there many of them?"

"Not many at all, I can tell you."

"And does it really make good soup?"

"Oh, wonderful soup! I'll tell you what. If you let me come in and lend me a pan, I'll show you."

"Yes, of course, do come in. I'll get you a pan right away."

So the man came in, and the woman got him the pan. He put the stone at the bottom, and covered it with plenty of water, and after a while it began to boil. The man stirred it, and peered at it, and began to hum a little. "Hmm, hmm, lovely, lovely soup," he said.

"Is it ready yet?" said the woman.

"Oh no, not yet," said the man. "But it's going to be gorgeous soup. I'll tell you what. Have you got such a thing as a carrot?"

"Yes, I have," said the woman.

"Well if we put it in the soup, it'll be even better," said the man. "It'll bring the full flavour out."

"All right," said the woman. "I'll get it." So she got the carrot and they put it in the soup.

The man stirred it, and peered at it, and hummed a bit, and pretty soon he said, "Tell you what. Have you got such a thing as an onion?"

"Would that make it better still?" asked the woman.

"Yes, it would," said the man. "It's gorgeous soup, but an onion would bring out the full flavour."

So they put an onion in the soup.

The man stirred it round, and hummed the way he did, and sniffed it and peered at it, and pretty soon he said, "I'll tell you what would be good now, to put in it. A chicken, and plenty of salt and pepper, of course."

"Oh, of course," said the woman. "I'll get that."

So they put in a chicken, and plenty of salt and pepper, and the man said the soup-stone soup would be very good indeed.

After an hour or two, they took out everything but the soup-stone, because the man said the soup was almost ready; they just needed the stone to boil a little longer to bring out the proper flavour.

Then, at last, the man lifted the stone out, and they served the soup. My, it *was* good! That soup-stone certainly made good soup!

"It's delicious!" said the woman. "How wonderful to have a stone that makes soup. I wish I had one like that."

"Well, there aren't many about, you know," said the man. "You can't get them easily."

"I don't suppose you can," said the woman. "But my, oh my, I certainly wish I could have one, and have soup like that all the time."

"Well, I'll tell you what," said the man. "Because you've been so kind to me, I'll give you mine, my very own soup-stone. Perhaps I'll be able to get hold of another."

"Oh, would you really?" said the woman. "It's very good of you. It will be wonderful to have a soup-stone and be for ever having soup."

So the man gave her his stone, and they said goodbye.

And when the poor man was hungry again, do you know what he did? He just bent down again, and picked up another stone, and said it was a soup-stone, and that was the way he managed every time.

THE
THIRTEEN
CATS

Daphne Lister

In a little house in a country village there lived an old lady who kept thirteen cats. There were black cats and ginger cats and grey cats and striped cats and one was a tortoiseshell and one was white all over. The whole house seemed to be *full* of cats, for they slept on the beds and they slept on the hearthrug and they slept on the windowsill. One – the white cat – even slept on top of a high cupboard!

People who went past the house could see cats sitting on the gate and cats sitting in the garden and cats sitting on the doorstep, and they said to each other, "The old woman must be a witch. Only a witch would keep so many cats."

And some people would say, "Yes, and she has thirteen and everyone knows thirteen is an unlucky number so she *must* be a witch."

No one ever went through the gate and up the path to the green front door – except the milkman who had to go and leave thirteen bottles of milk on the step every day.

The old lady was very happy in her little house with her thirteen cats but sometimes she wished she had some human friends as well. She didn't know that people thought she was a witch and were frightened of her.

One day a man and his wife and their son Tim moved into the cottage opposite. Now Tim had to spend his days in a wheelchair and couldn't run about and play with the other children, and because people felt rather shy when they saw him and didn't know what to say to him they often looked the other way. But Tim *did* make some friends, for when he wheeled himself across the road and stroked the old lady's ginger cat which was sitting on the gate, it purred loudly and came and sat on his lap. The next day the white cat did the same and the next day it was the turn of the tortoiseshell.

Soon Tim got to know all the cats and the old lady as well. She invited him to wheel his chair up the path to her little house and gave him home-made biscuits and cups of lemon tea. Sometimes Tim drew pictures of the cats and the old lady saw they were very good pictures and wished that she had some paints and coloured pencils and drawing paper to give him. But she hadn't much money because it costs a lot to buy thirteen bottles of milk every day.

Soon after harvest time there was a plague of rats in the village. They came to eat the grain in the farmers' barns and soon found their way into all the kitchens as well. Of course, there was *one* house they *didn't* go to and that was the old lady's. One look at all those cats and they ran off and left her in peace.

It wasn't long before everyone in the village was worried about the rats. "What shall we do?" they asked each other. One farmer knew what *he* was going to do. He was going to the old woman's to ask for help, witch or no witch.

The old woman was very surprised when she saw the farmer standing on her doorstep.

"Please, ma'am, I'd like to buy one of your cats to help me get rid of the rats in my barns and farmhouse," said the farmer.

"Oh, but I couldn't sell any of my cats," said the old lady. "You see, they are my family . . . but you could borrow one for a day or two."

"Thank you very much, ma'am," said the farmer. "I'm very grateful to you," and he put some coins on the table.

The old lady was just about to refuse the money when she had an idea, so she took it and said, "Thank you."

The farmer went away with one of the ginger cats and by next day news had got around that it had killed lots of rats.

By midday two more people had gone to the old lady's house to borrow cats and when Tim arrived the old lady asked him to make her a sign. Tim wrote "RENTACAT" in big letters on a piece of cardboard and the old lady fixed it to her gate.

In no time at all the villagers were queuing up for cats and handing the old lady their coins. So many people wanted cats that Tim had to make a waiting list.

In three weeks' time there wasn't a rat left in the village. Everyone was delighted, including the old lady. She used every penny she'd collected to buy drawing paper and crayons and paints and paintbrushes for Tim and he made even better pictures than before.

He and the old lady had lots and lots of friends because now that people had been to the old lady's house and got to know her they weren't frightened of her any more. And when they saw Tim's pictures they talked to him about them and forgot to feel shy because he was in a wheelchair.

And the cats were happy, too, because people were so grateful to them for chasing away the nasty rats that they often brought them little treats like tasty scraps of bacon!

RIP VAN WINKLE

Washington Irving
Retold by Fiona Waters

Everyone in the village loved Rip Van Winkle, except perhaps his poor wife. For although he was always ready to help a neighbour or show the children how to fly their kites or share a jar of ale with the other farmers, he was a lazy daydreamer at home. No matter how many times Dame Van Winkle reminded him to do his share of the work, their cow was always bellowing to be milked, the grass was overgrown, and the roof still leaked. Rip would just stick his fingers in his ears and disappear for a few hours, until it was safe to creep back, unnoticed, to play with his children in the dusty courtyard behind the farmhouse.

Now the village lay by the Hudson River at the foot of the Catskill Mountains. One day Rip decided to escape his wife's constant scolding to go hunting deep in the forest. He whistled to his faithful dog, Wolf, and the two of them set off up the mountain. By dusk Rip hadn't caught anything. He flung himself down on a mossy bank and closed his eyes, Wolf at his side. With a start he heard a ghostly voice calling his name, "Rip Van Winkle, Rip Van Winkle!" A low growl rose in Wolf's throat and a shiver ran down Rip's back. He ran his hand along Wolf's bristling fur and stood up.

"Perhaps it is someone who needs our help. Come on, Wolf. Let us see who is calling."

There in a clearing stood a small squat old man dressed in curiously old-fashioned clothes. He gestured towards a barrel at his feet and Rip realized the old man required him to lift it. The old man turned on his heel and walked down a path

leading deeper into the forest. As Rip bent to lift the heavy barrel he heard a strange sound like distant thunder rolling round the mountains.

The sun dipped behind the mountains as Rip and his silent companion walked into a deep valley that Rip had never seen before. Before his astonished eyes Rip saw a great number of ancient men, all dressed in the same strange clothes as his companion. They were playing ninepins and drinking from large earthenware mugs. With a thrill of fear, Rip remembered a painting he used to gaze at on the schoolroom wall, a painting of a famous explorer called Henry Hudson and the crew from his ship. He seemed to be looking at the same men. But how could that be? They had all been dead for many years!

The men motioned for Rip to open the barrel and they all filled their tankards before returning to their game. Boldness overcame his fear and, forgetting that he was already late getting home, Rip decided to try the ale for himself. The brew was heady and Rip found his eyes growing heavy. He lay down on the grass, conscious only that Wolf had disappeared before he fell into a deep sleep.

He awoke with a start to find the sun high in the sky. With a groan, Rip remembered the strong drink and realized that he had been out all night and that his poor wife would be worried and very angry indeed. He struggled to his feet, aware of a great stiffness in his bones, and looked round for Wolf. Then he shook his head in amazement. All his clothes were in rags and by his side, instead of his well-oiled gun, he found only a heap of rusty metal and crumbling wood! He turned towards the village and, coming across a stream, bent down to splash his face with water in a bid to clear his head. But whose was this old face with a grey beard reflected in the water before him? Now Rip was truly frightened.

"I have been bewitched!" he cried, and on shaking and tottery legs he ran all the way to the village. But everything had changed. When he finally found his house the roof had fallen in and weeds grew up through the courtyard. He ran into the street crying and tearing at his hair.

A young woman was passing and Rip went up to her in desperation and said, "Where is Dame Van Winkle, who used to live here?"

The young woman looked at him in bewilderment.

"Why, sir, my mother died twenty years ago!"

"Your mother?" said Rip. "Dame Van Winkle was my wife!"

The young woman looked confused and said, "Sir, I don't know who you are, but my father, Rip Van Winkle, went hunting with his dog, Wolf, many years ago and never returned."

By this time, what with all the commotion, quite a crowd had gathered.

The oldest man in the village came up close and peered at Rip, who seemed familiar.

"Well, well. It *is* Rip Van Winkle! Welcome home. Where have you been all these years?"

Rip repeated his fantastic tale of the mysterious sailors and their game of ninepins. All shook their heads in disbelief. But his daughter took pity on him and led him home with her. Rip spent the rest of his days smoking his pipe on her veranda with one of Wolf's descendants at his feet and teaching his grandchildren to fly kites. He never did understand what had happened to him that strange day all those years before. But whenever the thunder rolled round the Catskill Mountains, Rip Van Winkle would go inside and shut the door very firmly.

HAPPY BIRTHDAY, NANA BARBARA!

Pippa Goodhart

"Cock-a-doodle-doo!" called the cockerel. Nana Barbara opened one eye, then closed it again.

"I suppose that's your idea of a birthday present, is it? Waking me up early? Well, Mr Cockerel, you might cock-a-doodle-doo, but I cock-a-doodle-*don't* want to get up. A birthday on your own is no fun."

Nana Barbara turned over in bed and pulled up her covers. Mossy Cat came close and warm against her back. Nana Barbara reached out a hand to tickle Mossy behind the ears, and she told her, "When I was a little girl, birthdays used to be such special days, Mossy. They were presents-and surprises-days. One year my father hid all my presents and I had to follow clues to find them, as you would in a treasure hunt. Another year I had my birthday tea in a tree house that he and mother

83

had made. And there was always jelly, and there were family and friends, and my mother always wore an apron over her best dress when she brought in the cake glowing with candles. Then everyone would sing,

Happy Birthday to you,
Happy Birthday to you,
Happy Birthday, dear Barbara,
Happy Birthday to you!"

Nana Barbara sat up in bed and took the cat on to her lap. "Oh, Mossy, it was always special. I wished for the same thing year after year when I blew out my candles. Do you know what that was?"

"Miaow," said Mossy.

"I wished for a kitten, but I could never have one because cats made my brother sneeze."

A sound of hens came through the window. Cluck-cluck-cluck. Nana Barbara chuckled as she got out of bed. "You're quite right, you hens! I have been a clucky lucky lady and I shouldn't feel so sorry for myself."

Mossy licked a paw and stroked it over and over her head while Nana Barbara dressed herself and talked.

"I grew up and married a marvellous man, Mossy. He gave me a kitten. He made me cakes on my birthday and sang me 'Happy Birthday, my

sweetheart' in his deep wobbly voice. Then we had children and they sang 'Happy Birthday, dear Mummy'. And now I'm Nana Barbara to three grandsons and a baby granddaughter." Nana Barbara smiled. "But they are all too far away to sing to me today."

Nana Barbara pulled a jumper over her head and you could see her elbow through the sleeve.

"Bother!" said Nana Barbara. "It's got a hole. I shall mend it later, but first you want breakfast, don't you, Mossy? And our friends outside do, too."

Nana Barbara filled her wheelbarrow with hay

and bowls of grain and a full watering can, and she pushed it to the chicken run. "Here you are, my clucky lucky hen friends. And you, too, Mr Cockerel!" She filled their bowls and collected three warm eggs from the straw. "Eggs for my birthday breakfast. Thank you, hens!"

Nana Barbara went to the duck pen and threw grain on the grass, where the ducks waddle-quack gobbled it up. There were two beautiful blue-white eggs in the duck house. "The best eggs in the world for baking," said Nana Barbara. "I think perhaps I'll make myself a birthday cake. Thank you, my deary ducks!"

Nana Barbara pushed the wheelbarrow over to the sheepfold and poured food into the sheep's trough. "There you are, my woolly friends. Now the weather's warm it's time I sheared off all that wool of yours. Then I'll have wool to colour and spin and knit into a new jumper with no holes at the elbow. That'll be a lovely birthday present. Thank you, my dears!"

The goat came and gently butted Nana Barbara so that she dropped her armful of hay. "And you'll give me fresh milk for my birthday feast, will you, my funny friend?" As Nana Barbara settled on to a stool and began to milk the goat, Mossy came grinning and purring and rubbing around her legs. "And you, my dear Mossy, are with me, loving me all day every day, and there's no better present than that. Really, I'm a very lucky lady."

Nana Barbara ate her breakfast and baked her cake. She sheared the sheep and she picked golden crocus flowers and put them in a vase. "They can be my birthday candles," she said. She put the flowers and cake and milk on to a tray, and she took it out into the sunshine. "I'll have my birthday party out here with my animal friends. It will be just like a proper party, except, of course, there'll be no birthday song today." But then Nana Barbara suddenly laughed as she heard,

> *Miaow, quack, cluck, doodle-doo,*
> *Miaow, quack, cluck, doodle-doo,*
> *Miaow, quack, cluck, Naa Naa Baa Baa,*
> *Miaow, quack, cluck, doodle-doo!*

"Oh, my dears!" chuckled Nana Barbara. "I shall cut my cake and share it with you all, just as I shared my birthday cake with my friends in the old days."

The cat and the hens and the ducks and the sheep and the goat all enjoyed the cake very much. And so did Nana Barbara.

KEEPING WARMTH IN A BAG

A Native American tale
retold by Fiona Waters

It was always winter. Many, many moons ago the land was covered in deep, deep snow and the sun was never seen. The animals were all desperately cold and there was hardly any food. They gathered together in a great council, the birds of the air, the four-legged beasts of the land and even the mysterious creatures from the depths of the seas, to decide what to do. They talked and talked for three days and then they talked some more. After all this talking they were agreed that winter was lasting too long. Then they talked for another three days and then they talked some more. After all this talking they were agreed that winter was lasting too long because there was no warmth anywhere.

One wise caribou then said, "My friends, do you notice there are no bears in this council?"

The animals murmured among themselves and realized that in fact no one had seen any bears for years.

"Maybe the bears have stolen the warmth for themselves," growled the wolf. "We should go and find out."

So the caribou, the wolf, the bobcat, the mouse and the pike set off to find a hole in the sky – for the bears lived in another world high above the earth, beyond the clouds. Before too long they found one and all slipped through it into this other world. They walked for a time until they found a fire burning in front of a cave by the shore of a lake. Snuggled up beside the fire they found two bear cubs.

"Where is your mother?" the bobcat asked.

"She is out hunting," replied the bear cubs.

The mouse was sniffing round the cave and found several great bags hanging from the ceiling.

"What is in these bags, little cubs?" asked the mouse.

"Our mother keeps the weather in those," replied the cubs.

The bobcat pointed to the first one. "What is in here?"

"Rain," replied the cubs.

The wolf pointed to the second one. "And in here?"

"Our mother keeps the fog in that one," replied the cubs.

The mouse pointed to the third one. "What does your mother keep in this bag, please?"

"That bag is full of the winds," said the cubs.

The caribou nodded towards the fourth bag. "And in that bag, little ones?"

"We can't tell you that," said the cubs. "That is a secret. Our mother told us not to tell anyone what is in there."

"But we are all friends here," said the caribou. "Tell us what is in that bag, little ones."

The cubs whispered together and then said, "Well, as we are all friends, we can tell you that bag is full of warmth."

"Ahhh!" said the caribou, the wolf, the bobcat, the mouse and the pike all together. "Thank you, little cubs, you have told us all we needed to know."

Just then they heard the sound of the mother bear striding through the forest on her way home. So the animals all rushed outside and hid some way off to have another council to decide how best to take the bag of warmth back to earth with them.

But the mother bear spotted the caribou trying to hide behind a rock and she called to her cubs, "Quick, my little ones! Help me catch this caribou. He will make a very good dinner for us." So the cubs scrambled up from the fireside and chased after their mother, forgetting that the caribou was supposed to be a friend.

The caribou called over his shoulder to the other animals, "I will try to lead the bear away from the cave and tire her out. You must all grab the bag of warmth and carry it as fast as you can to the hole in the sky, where I will join you."

And so it happened. The caribou ran as fast as the wind towards the far side of the lake, the bears in close pursuit. At the same moment the animals dashed into the cave and grabbed the bag containing warmth. It was very heavy and, of course, very hot, so it was difficult to carry and they were soon exhausted. The caribou had now run right round the lake and was heading back towards the cave with the bears growling at his heels. It looked as if all was lost. The pike then cried, "I will lure the mother bear into the lake to give you more time," and he dived deep into the lake just as the bear splashed into the water. The pike swam round and round in circles so the bear was soon too dizzy to know what was going on.

The relieved caribou joined his friends as they pushed the heavy bag through the opening in the sky. At the very last moment the pike leapt up out of the water and, following the other animals, slipped through the hole to the world below.

They opened the bag as soon as ever possible and the sun came out. The wonderful warmth spread in every direction and the snow all melted. This, of course, caused a great flood – but that is another story!

EGGS

Joan Aiken

"Oh, how I wish I had an alarm clock," sighed Mrs Smith each morning. "Every single day little Sam is late for school, and William is late for work."

William, her husband, took no notice of this. He was spraying his roses. Nothing but roses grew in Mr Smith's garden, which lay right by the road. People walking along could lean over the low wooden fence and breathe in the scent, which was like warm Madeira cake mixed with raspberry trifle. And they could gaze at the gorgeous colours of flowers, red, white, pink, flame, yellow and orange. People walked very slowly along that stretch of road. Bees hummed among the roses all day; they came from all over the country to make honey from Mr Smith's roses. And from March to November Mr Smith spent every free hour in his garden, watering, digging, raking the ground, picking off dead flowers, pruning, and spraying the roses and plants to get rid of greenfly, caterpillars, and nibbling insects.

There wasn't any room for little Sam in the garden. *He* had to play on the cement strip by the back door. And he would have liked a kitten, or maybe a puppy, but his father said animals would damage the flowers.

Every day little Sam was late for school because his father, who drove him there, had to be called in from the garden where he was caring for his roses; and every day Mr Smith was late for his job in the garden shop where he worked, selling roses and mowers and wheelbarrows.

Mr Smith liked working in the garden shop because he could get rose plants at half price.

"Hurry, William!" cried his wife. "You'll be late! And Sam will be late for school. Here're your sandwiches, Sam, and your school bag. And, William, will you *please* buy me an alarm clock, so we can all get up earlier in the morning?"

"If I remember," said Mr Smith. But she knew he would not remember. He would just buy another rose plant.

Father and son were leaving by the back door, to get to the shed where Mr Smith kept his old pick-up, when, guess what happened! With a crash louder than eighty tons of boulders falling on an ice rink, a lorry skidded off the road – across the pavement – through the wooden fence – and straight into Mr Smith's garden, ploughing over the roses, and ending up with its radiator jammed into the next-door fence. Then it fell on its side, because Mr Smith's garden was on quite a steep slope.

If Mr Smith had stayed in his garden *one minute* longer he would have been run over too, along with his roses!

"Mercy!" cried Mrs Smith, running out of the back door. "*Mercy*, what's happened? Sam! William! Are you all right?"

"Oh, my lord! Oh, my roses!" wailed Mr Smith.

For the roses that had not been mashed by the truck were now completely buried under its load, which had tumbled out all over the garden.

What was that load?

Eggs! The truck had been taking forty thousand eggs to a cake factory. And every single one was now lying smashed all over Mr Smith's rose bed.

"What *happened*?" Mrs Smith asked the driver, who had clambered down, gulping and trembling, from his cab.

"A bee stung me, that's what! Made me swerve."

"I'll want compensation for this," moaned

Mr Smith, looking at his ruined rose bed. "Compensation! My roses would have taken all the prizes at the County Show tomorrow."

"My firm will pay you," said the driver.

"Maybe, we can buy an alarm clock with the money," said Mrs Smith. But she didn't really believe so. She knew the money would go to buy more rose plants. "Look at all those broken eggs! Not a whole one among them. What a shame! What a waste!"

The garden was bright yellow, and all gooey. Little Sam was up to his knees in egg yolk.

"Sam, come out of that! *Look* at you!"

But Sam called, "Hey, Ma, look what I found! One egg isn't broken. Just one! Can I have it?" he

asked the driver, who was limping indoors to phone for the breakdown service.

"Help yourself, son. No one's going to count those eggs . . ."

As Sam gently held the egg in his hand, he felt something alive, moving about inside it.

"Oh! It made a noise!

There's a live chick in there! Ma, can I keep it? Can I hatch it?"

"Dad doesn't want chickens in the garden," began Mrs Smith. But then she looked at the ruined roses and said, "Oh, what's the difference? Put it in a basket by the stove where it'll keep warm. Now, clean yourself up for school. I never did *see* such a sight —"

"Egg yolks must be good for the ground," sighed Mr Smith.

When little Sam came home at tea time, the egg in the basket was beginning to bump and joggle about. And then, crack! It opened. Out crawled a damp and yellow chick.

"Give it a spoonful of cereal," said Sam's mother. "And a drink of water."

Soon the chick was dry, and yellow and fluffy.

"I'll call him Herbert," said Sam.

"Perhaps it's a hen," said his mother.

But Herbert was a cock. Long before Mr Smith had dug in the broken eggshells, and before the new roses were planted and blooming, Herbert had grown into a splendid rooster. He had a scarlet comb, black and green tail feathers, a gold-brown chest, and orange legs with black feather breeches. He followed Sam everywhere, sat beside him on the new patch of grass that had been planted, and ate all the slugs and snails in the garden.

And, every morning, sharp at half-past six, he shouted: "Cock-a-doodle-doo! Time to get up! Cock-a-doodle-doo!"

Never again did Mrs Smith need to wish for an alarm clock. Or Sam for a kitten.

BRER RABBIT
TO THE RESCUE

Julius Lester

Brer Fox was coming from town one evening when he saw Brer Turtle. He thought this was as good a time as any to grab Brer Rabbit's best friend.

He was close to home so he ran, got a sack, and ran back, knowing Brer Turtle wouldn't have covered more than two or three feet of ground.

Brer Fox didn't even say how-do like the animals usually did, but just reached down, grabbed Brer Turtle, and flung him in the sack. Brer Turtle squalled and kicked and screamed. Brer Fox tied a knot in the sack and headed for home.

Brer Rabbit was lurking around Brer Fox's watermelon patch, wondering how he was going to get one, when he heard Brer Fox coming, singing like he'd just discovered happiness. Brer Rabbit jumped into a ditch and hid.

"I wonder what's in that sack Brer Fox got slung over his shoulder?" Brer Rabbit wondered. He wondered and he wondered, and the more he wondered, the more he didn't know. He knew this much: Brer Fox had absolutely no business walking up the road singing and carrying something which nobody but him knew what it was.

Brer Rabbit went up to his house and yelled, "Hey, Brer Fox! Brer Fox! Come quick! There's a whole crowd of folks down in your watermelon patch. They carrying off watermelons and tromping on your vines like it's a holiday or something! I tried to get 'em out, but they ain't gon' pay a little man like me no mind. You better hurry!"

Brer Fox dashed out. Brer Rabbit chuckled and went inside. He looked around until he saw the sack in the corner. He picked it up and felt it.

"Let me alone!" came a voice from inside. "Turn me loose! You hear me?"

Brer Rabbit dropped the sack and jumped back. Then he laughed. "Only one man in the world can make a fuss like that and that's Brer Turtle."

"Brer Rabbit? That you?"

"It was when I got up this morning."

"Get me out of here. I got dust in my throat and grit in my eye and I can't breathe none too good either. Get me out, Brer Rabbit."

"Tell me one thing, Brer Turtle. I can figure out how you got in the sack, but I can't for the life of me figure how you managed to tie a knot in it after you was inside."

Brer Turtle wasn't in the mood for none of Brer Rabbit's joking. "If you don't get me out of this sack, I'll tell your wife about all the time you spend with Miz Meadows and the girls."

Brer Rabbit untied the sack in a hurry. He carried Brer Turtle out to the woods and looked around for a while.

"What you looking for, Brer Rabbit?"

"There it is!" Brer Rabbit exclaimed.

He took a hornet's nest down from a tree and stuffed the opening with leaves. Then he took the nest to Brer Fox's house and put it in the sack. He tied the sack tightly, then picked it up, flung it at the wall, dropped it on the floor, and swung it over his head a couple of times to get the hornets stirred up good. Then he put the sack back in the corner and ran to the woods where Brer Turtle was hiding.

A few minutes later Brer Fox came up the road, and he was angry! He stormed in the house. Brer Rabbit and Brer Turtle waited. All of a sudden they heard chairs falling, dishes breaking, the table turning over. It sounded like a bunch of cows was loose in the house.

Brer Fox came tearing through the door – and he hadn't even stopped to open it. The hornets were on him like a second skin.

Yes, that was one day Brer Fox found out what pain and suffering is all about.

MILLY-MOLLY-MANDY GOES BLACKBERRYING

Joyce Lankester Brisley

Once upon a time Milly-Molly-Mandy found some big ripe blackberries on her way home from school. There were six great beauties and one little hard one, so Milly-Molly-Mandy put the little hard one in her mouth and carried the others home on a leaf.

She gave one to Father, and Father said, "Ah! That makes me think the time for blackberry puddings has come!"

Then she gave one to Mother, and asked what it made her think of. And Mother said, "A whole row of pots of blackberry jam that I ought to have in my store-cupboard!"

Then she gave one to Grandpa, and Grandpa said it made him think "Blackberry tart!"

And Grandma said, "Blackberry jelly!"

And Uncle said, "Stewed blackberry-and-apple!"

And Aunty said, "A plate of blackberries with sugar and cream!"

"My!" thought Milly-Molly-Mandy, as she threw away the empty leaf, "I must get a big, big basket and go blackberrying the very next Saturday, so that there can be lots of puddings and jam and tarts and jelly and stewed blackberry-and-apple and fresh blackberries, for Farver and Muvver and Grandpa and Grandma and Uncle and Aunty – and me! I'll ask Susan to come too."

So the very next Saturday Milly-Molly-Mandy and little-friend-Susan set out with big baskets (to hold the blackberries) and hooked sticks (to pull the brambles nearer) and stout boots (to keep the prickles off) and old frocks (lest the thorns should catch). And they walked and they walked, till they came to a place where they knew there was always a lot of blackberries – at the proper time of year, of course.

But when they came to the place – oh, dear! – they saw a notice-board stuck up just inside a gap in the fence. And the notice-board said, as plain as anything:

TRESPASSERS
WILL BE
PROSECUTED

Milly-Molly-Mandy and little-friend-Susan knew that meant "You mustn't come here, because the owner doesn't want you and it's his land."

Milly-Molly-Mandy and little-friend-Susan looked at each other very solemnly indeed. Then Milly-Molly-Mandy said, "I don't s'pose anyone would see if we went in."

And little-friend-Susan said, "I don't s'pose they'd miss any of the blackberries."

And Milly-Molly-Mandy said, "But it wouldn't be right."

And little-friend-Susan shook her head very firmly.

So they took up their baskets and sticks and moved away, trying not to feel hurt about it, although they had come a long way to that place.

They didn't know quite what to do with themselves after that, for there seemed to be no blackberries anywhere else, so they amused themselves by walking in a dry ditch close by the fence, shuffling along in the leaves with their stout little boots that were to have kept the prickles off.

And suddenly – what do you think they saw? A little ball of brown fur, just ahead of them among the grasses in the ditch.

"Is it a rabbit?" whispered little-friend-Susan. They crept closer.

"It is a rabbit!" whispered Milly-Molly-Mandy.

"Why doesn't it run away?" said little-friend-Susan, and she stroked it. The little ball of fur wriggled. Then Milly-Molly-Mandy stroked it, and it wriggled again.

Then Milly-Molly-Mandy exclaimed, "I believe it's got its head stuck in a hole in the bank!"

And they looked, and that was just what had happened. Some earth had fallen down as bunny was burrowing, and it couldn't get its head out again.

So Milly-Molly-Mandy and little-friend-Susan carefully dug with their fingers, and loosened the earth round about, and as soon as bunny's head was free he shook his ears and stared at them.

Milly-Molly-Mandy and little-friend-Susan sat very still, and only smiled and nodded gently to show him he needn't be afraid, because they loved him.

And then little bunny turned his head and ran skitter-scutter along the ditch and up the bank, into the wood and was gone.

"Oh!" said Milly-Molly-Mandy, "we always wanted a rabbit, and now we've got one, Susan!"

"Only we'd rather ours played in the fields with his brothers and sisters instead of stopping in a poky hutch," said little-friend-Susan.

"And if we'd gone trespassing we should never have come here and found him," said Milly-Molly-Mandy. "I'd much rather have a little rabbit than a whole lot of blackberries."

And when they got back to the nice white cottage with the thatched roof, where Milly-Molly-Mandy lived, Father and Mother and Grandpa and Grandma and Uncle and Aunty all said they would much rather have a little rabbit running about in the woods than all the finest blackberries in the world.

However, the next Saturday Milly-Molly-Mandy and little-friend-Susan came upon a

splendid place for blackberrying, without any notice-board; and Milly-Molly-Mandy gathered such a big basketful that there was enough to make blackberry puddings and jam and tarts and jelly and stewed blackberry-and-apple and fresh blackberries for Father and Mother and Grandpa and Grandma and Uncle and Aunty – and Milly-Molly-Mandy too.

And all the time a little rabbit skipped about in the woods and thought what a lovely world it was. (And that's a true story!)

ALLY BALLY AND THE MAGIC BAG

Tony Mitton

Ally Bally was on his way back from market. He was trying to carry all the things he had bought, but he kept dropping them.

"I wish I'd brought a bag," he sighed.

"A bag, did you say?"

Ally looked around to see where the voice had come from.

"Over here," said the voice. "Under the palm tree."

Ally looked and saw a little round man in a brightly coloured turban. He was holding up a grubby brown bag for Ally to see.

"It may not look much, but it will hold all your shopping for you. Go on, take it," said the man.

Ally looked at the bag. Then he looked at his shopping on the ground.

"Thank you," he said. "I will."

119

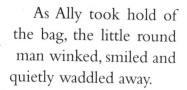

As Ally took hold of the bag, the little round man winked, smiled and quietly waddled away.

Ally was just about to pick up his shopping when he heard another voice.

"Magic bag, magic bag, never a bulge, no, never a sag."

"Who said that?" gasped Ally, dropping the bag. He looked around, but there was nobody there.

"Put things in, put things in, light as a feather, neat as a pin."

Ally suddenly realized that the words were coming from the bag itself.

"A talking bag!" cried Ally with delight. "What fun! Maybe it will talk again soon. How nice to have some company."

As Ally packed his shopping, the bag didn't get any fuller or heavier. All of the things he put in just seemed to vanish. It was as if the bag was gobbling them up like a greedy monster.

"That's very strange," thought Ally. But he set off home with the bag slung lightly over his shoulder.

Before long Ally came to a bend in the road. As he went round it he bumped right into a big, bad brigand. The brigand looked very fierce.

"What's in the bag?" he growled. "Show me!"

"Only sh-sh-shopping," stammered Ally. "Nothing valuable. I'm just a poor farmer."

"I'll see for myself," said the brigand, grabbing hold of the bag. As he did so it began to whisper to him, *"Jewels and gold, jewels and gold, all the treasure you can hold."*

"Oh-o!" shouted the brigand. And he pulled the mouth of the bag open and thrust his head in to look.

"I wouldn't do that if I were you," said Ally nervously. But it was too late. The bag had begun to gobble up the brigand.

"Help, help, help!" came the brigand's shouts from inside. But in went his feet and the bag shut tightly.

To Ally's astonishment, the bag seemed just as light and empty as before. He didn't really know what to do next, so he just set off on his way again.

"When I get home I'll think of what to do about the brigand," he said to himself.

But he had not gone far when galloping down the road came two of the Sultan's soldiers.

"Someone has stolen the Sultan's jewels," they shouted. "Everyone has to be searched. Open your bag and let us see inside."

"Oh, dear," said Ally. "I don't think that would be very wise."

"What are you trying to hide?" shouted the soldiers impatiently. "Open the bag at once or we shall have to arrest you."

"Oh, do be careful," said Ally. "Mind the . . ."

But the soldiers had whisked the bag out of his hands and were peering into its mouth. As Ally watched, he saw it open to gobble up both soldiers and their fine white horses too. There he stood, alone on the empty road, with only the bag at his feet.

"Whatever next?" sighed Ally. And he slung the bag over his shoulder and set off again, puzzling as he went.

By the time Ally got home he was feeling rather hungry.

"But my food is in the bag," he wailed. "However will I get it out?"

He reached very carefully into the bag and began to feel around. "That feels like an onion," he said, gripping on to something round and bulbous. So he pulled and pulled and pulled until out plopped the brigand on to the ground in front of him. Ally was still holding the brigand's nose.

"Make a fool of me, would you?" screamed the brigand. "When I've found out what you have in this crazy bag, I'll deal with *you*." And he grabbed the bag and thrust a strong arm in to feel around inside. "Aha," he cried. "Now *this* feels like treasure." So he pulled and pulled and pulled until out plopped one soldier and then the other and both of their horses behind them. The brigand was grasping on to one of their small, round shields.

"Try to ambush us, would you?" growled the soldier to the brigand. "We'll soon see about that."

"Look!" gasped the other soldier. "He is wearing one of the Sultan's jewels. He must be the thief."

As they searched his many pockets, they soon found all of the stolen jewels.

"Well done, young man," said the first soldier to Ally. "There'll be a big reward for this. Follow us to the palace. The Sultan will wish to thank you for himself."

As the soldiers led the thief away, Ally looked to see what had become of the bag. The shopping was there, but the bag – it was gone. Then, off in the

distance, just going round a bend in the road, he noticed a little round man in a brightly coloured turban. Ally smiled.

"If I am to have a big reward, I'll need something to carry it in," he said to himself. And this time he made sure to take his biggest and best shopping bag.

THERE'S NO SUCH THING AS A FAIRY...

Simon Puttock

Zelda had a wobbly tooth. It was her first wobbly tooth *ever*. She wiggled and jiggled and poked it with her tongue. Sometimes she wiggled and jiggled and poked too hard, and said, "Ow!"

Dad was reading Zelda a story to take her mind off her tooth.

"'And all the lovely little fairies lived happily ever after,'" said Dad, closing the book. "Did you like that story, Zelda?" he asked.

"Ow!" said Zelda, jiggling away. "It was all right, but . . . you know, Dad, there aren't *really* any such things as fairies."

"No such thing as fairies?" asked Dad, surprised. "Are you sure? What about the fairies at the bottom of the garden?"

"Dad," said Zelda sternly, "there *aren't* any fairies at the bottom of the garden. There's just *garden*."

127

Zelda was going to be a scientist when she grew up. Scientists, she knew, were interested in *real* things. Zelda had lots of clever books that explained all about spaceships and dinosaurs and bugs. But *not* fairies. Because there is no such thing as a fairy.

"Are you *very* sure?" asked Dad.

"Very sure," said Zelda. "I will show you." And she took Dad down to the bottom of the garden. "There," she said. "See? NO FAIRIES!"

"Ah," said Dad. "There are no fairies that we can *see*, but they might be hiding. A fairy might be hiding under that leaf."

Zelda looked under the leaf. There wasn't a fairy, but there was a hairy caterpillar.

"Caterpillars," Zelda explained, "turn into butterflies with beautiful, bright wings. But butterflies are *not* fairies."

"I see," said Dad. "What about behind that rock?"

Zelda looked behind the rock. There wasn't a fairy, but there was a bunchy brown spider.

"Spiders," Zelda explained, "have eight legs and lots of eyes. They can fly through the air on threads of gossamer. But spiders are *definitely* not fairies."

"Naturally," said Dad. "But how about under that log?"

Zelda looked under the log. There wasn't a fairy, but there was a shy snail.

"Snails," said Zelda, "have eyes that stick out on stalks and one big, floppy foot. They leave trails of shiny silver wherever they go. But snails are not now, nor have they *ever been,* fairies."

"How true," agreed Dad.

Zelda and Dad looked in the long grass. They looked under a bit of old bark. They even looked inside a flower. They found a bright red ladybird with seven black spots. They found a grumpy woodlouse that curled into a ball. They even found a bee, busy gathering nectar. But there weren't any fairies.

And all the while, Zelda wiggled and jiggled and poked at her tooth.

"You see," she said, "there are *no such things* as fairies – Ow!"

Out of her mouth popped the wobbly tooth, and it plopped on to the grass.

"Well done!" said Dad. "Does it hurt?"

"Not really," said Zelda, feeling the new, soft gummy bit with her tongue. It felt interesting. Then she smiled a big gappy smile.

"You know," said Dad thoughtfully, "it really is a pity that there *aren't* any fairies. Because if there *were*, you could put that tooth under your pillow tonight and the tooth fairy would come and take it, and leave a nice shiny pound in its place."

"Dad," said Zelda. "There are NO SUCH THINGS AS —"

Zelda's mouth popped shut. Her scientific brain thought hard. A whole pound! Wow! She had *never* had a whole pound before. There are *lots* of things you can do with a pound. Zelda made a scientific decision.

"You know what, Dad?" she said. "The thing about scientists is, they have to keep an *open mind* about stuff. And they have to do *experiments*, to find things out. So I think I *will* put my tooth under my pillow after all. Just as an experiment, of course. Just to see what happens. Just to keep an open mind. Because – you *never know!*"

THE HUNTED HARE

An English folk tale
retold by Ethel Johnston Phelps

Once upon a time there was an old woman who lived by herself on the edge of the great wild moor. Many tales the folk thereabouts told were of evil spirits, and all manner of fearful things that roamed the moor at night. You may be sure they took care never to be abroad on that bleak stretch of lonely land once darkness had fallen.

Now it happened the old woman had to cross the moor once a week to reach the market town to sell her butter and eggs. She usually rose early, just before dawn, to set out. One night, knowing the next day to be market day, she went to bed quite early. When she awoke, she began to get ready for her journey. It was still dark of course, and, having no clock, she did not know it was still before midnight. She dressed, ate, saddled her horse, and attached to it the large wicker panniers containing the butter and eggs. Wrapping a worn old cloak about her, she and the horse sleepily set off across the moor.

She had not gone very far before she heard the sounds of a pack of hounds baying under the stars and saw, racing towards her, a white hare. When it reached her, the hare leapt up on a large rock close by the path as if to say, "Come, catch me."

The old woman chuckled. She liked the idea of outwitting the hounds, so she reached out her hand, picked up the crouching hare, and popped it into one of her wicker panniers. She dropped the lid and rode on.

The baying of the hounds came nearer, and suddenly she saw a headless horse galloping towards her, surrounded by a pack of monstrous hounds. On the horse sat a dark figure. The eyes of the hounds shone fiery red, while their tails glowed with a blue flame.

It was a terrifying sight to behold. Her horse stood trembling and shaking, but the woman sat up boldly to confront the rider. She had the hare in her basket and didn't intend to give it up. But it seemed that these monstrous creatures were not very clever or knowing, for the rider asked the old woman, very civilly, had she seen a white hare run past and did she know in which direction it had gone.

"No indeed," she said firmly. "I saw no hare run past me." Which of course was true.

The rider spurred his headless horse, called his hounds to follow, and galloped across the moors. When they were out of sight, the woman patted and calmed her shivering horse.

Suddenly, to her surprise, the lid of the pannier moved and then opened. It was no frightened hare who came forth, but a woman all in white.

The ghostly lady spoke in a clear voice. "Dame," she said, "I admire your courage. You have saved me from a terrible enchantment and now the spell is broken. I am no human woman – it was my fate to be condemned for centuries to the form of a hare

and to be pursued on the moor at night by evil spirits, until I could get behind their tails while they passed on in search of me. Through your courage the enchantment is broken, and I can now return to my own kind. We will never forget you. I promise that all your hens shall lay two eggs instead of one, your cows shall give plenty of milk year round, your garden crops shall thrive and yield a fine harvest. But beware the rider and his evil spirits, for he will try to do you harm once he realizes you were clever enough to outwit him. May good fortune attend you."

The mysterious lady vanished and was never seen again, but all she promised came true. The woman had the best possible luck at market that morning and continued to have good fortune with all her crops and livestock. The rider never did succeed in getting revenge and the kindly protection of the ghostly lady stayed with the woman the rest of her life.

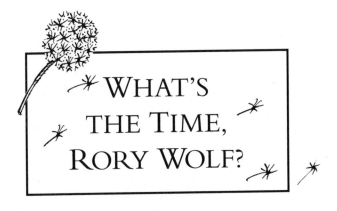

WHAT'S THE TIME, RORY WOLF?

Gillian McClure

High on a windy mountain in a forest that clung to a slope, lived a wolf called Rory. The forest had grown dismal and gloomy since Rory Wolf had made it his home.

At first it had been full of birds, animals and flowers. But Rory Wolf had eaten them all. He had gobbled up his enemies first and then when winters were harsh and food scarce he had turned on his friends and neighbours too. Now there was nothing left in the forest except Rory Wolf, a very lonely and hungry wolf.

A little way down the mountain was a village. Rory Wolf found a rubbish dump outside it and enough food to stay alive. But he wanted more than food, he wanted friends.

"Where can a wolf find a friend?" he howled.

Up the mountain he saw only cold stars shining

on the wild windswept slopes, but down the mountain he saw the village and warm lamplight glowing in the windows.

"More life down there," he growled.

So early the next day Rory Wolf smartened up his shaggy coat and practised a smile in the pond's mirror.

"Now I can look quite nice when I try, perhaps I can *be* nice, too," he snapped at the fishes. But they laughed big bubbles at him from the bottom of the pond where they knew they were safe.

Rory Wolf set off down towards the village and on the way he met a little old woman. Rory Wolf liked little old women because they reminded him of Red Riding Hood's granny.

"Excuse me, my good old woman," Rory Wolf meant to say, but the cold air had made his voice gruff and growly.

"Ahhhhhhhhhhhhh!" gasped the old woman.

"Ugh! Ugh! Ugh!" coughed the wolf.

"Help!" cried the old woman.

"Arrrrrrrrrrr!" wheezed the wolf.

"Wolf!" screamed the old woman. "Wolf, wolf!" she screeched and ran down the road on her old creaking legs.

Rory Wolf was surprised and a little taken aback.

"What's wrong? I'm not a snappy wolf and I'm certainly not a snarly wolf."

A little further on Rory Wolf saw a fisherman. Rory Wolf loved fish; he would have liked to have been a fisherman himself but was far too fidgety to catch fish.

"Any luck?" growled the wolf, his mouth watering.

"Ooooooh!" shouted the fisherman.

"Got a fish?" asked the wolf excitedly.

"Splash!" went the fisherman.

"Water cold?" growled the wolf, surprised.

"Ssssssssssssplutter!" went the fisherman, going under and surfacing again further downstream.

Rory Wolf was puzzled and a little hurt. "What's wrong? I'm not a wicked wolf and I'm certainly not a wilful wolf."

And Rory Wolf went on his way.

He reached the village and heard a band playing. Rory Wolf missed music, for no bird ever sang in his forest now.

"Bravo!" roared the wolf.

The music suddenly stopped.

"Encore!" roared the wolf.

"Rrrrrrrrumpa CRASH!" went the drummer and drum.

"Let's have a fox-trot," growled the wolf.

"Ooooompah pah BANG!" went the big bassoon.

"Who will dance with *me*?" howled the wolf.

"Ting ting CRACK!" went the small triangle and the whole band leapt from the stand.

Rory Wolf felt snubbed and a little peeved.

"What's wrong? I'm not a mangy wolf and I'm certainly not a smelly wolf! Perhaps there's something wrong with them," and Rory Wolf turned to go back to his forest.

But before he had gone very far he saw some children playing 'What's the time, Mr Wolf?' That was Rory Wolf's favourite game and he crept up behind them and roared out, "DINNER TIME!"

The children scattered ...

All, that is, except one girl called Charlotte. She did not mind wolves and just stood and stared at Rory Wolf.

"I only wanted to be friends," puffed the wolf.

"All right," said Charlotte. "But you won't eat me, will you?"

"Do I look as if I would?" asked the wolf with a long and hungry sigh.

So Charlotte and Rory Wolf became friends and enjoyed all kinds of rough gruff games together. They played leapfrog and tig and Roly Poly Rory

down the hill. But the exercise made the wolf hungry, so hungry he forgot he was trying to be nice.

"Why not come back to the forest with me and play 'Who's afraid of the big bad wolf?'" he suggested.

But Charlotte thought she should ask her parents first.

Her mother was frightened. "Don't you ever see that wolf again," she shouted. "Remember the story of *Little Red Riding Hood*!"

This made Rory Wolf ashamed; he blamed his mistake on his empty tummy.

Then Charlotte's father got down his gun.

Rory Wolf thought, "I'd better run. I can see this friendship coming to a quick and nasty end!" And he shot off into the night.

Charlotte missed Rory Wolf so much that her father was forced to buy her a large dog.

"To take her mind off wolves," said her mother.

"To chase the blighters away," said her father.

Charlotte called her dog Rory.

As for Rory Wolf, he missed Charlotte, too, though he carried on his search for a friend, this time climbing high on to the wild windswept mountain. And at last he did find a friend; another wolf like himself. Now Rory Wolf is not lonely any more; he lives in a den on the top of the mountain with his mate and their cub, which Rory Wolf calls Charlotte.

How the Camel Got His Hump

Rudyard Kipling

Now this is the next tale, and it tells how the Camel got his big hump.

In the beginning of years, when the world was so new-and-all, and the Animals were just beginning to work for Man, there was a Camel, and he lived in the middle of a Howling Desert because he did not want to work; and besides, he was a Howler himself. So he ate sticks and thorns and tamarisks and milkweed and prickles, most 'scruciating idle; and when anybody spoke to him he said "Humph!" Just "Humph!" and no more.

Presently the Horse came to him on Monday morning, with a saddle on his back and a bit in his mouth, and said, "Camel, O Camel, come out and trot like the rest of us."

"Humph!" said the Camel; and the Horse went away and told the Man.

Presently the Dog came to him, with a stick in his mouth, and said, "Camel, O Camel, come and fetch and carry like the rest of us."

"Humph!" said the Camel; and the Dog went away and told the Man.

Presently the Ox came to him, with the yoke on his neck, and said, "Camel, O Camel, come and plough like the rest of us."

"Humph!" said the Camel; and the Ox went away and told the Man.

At the end of the day the Man called the Horse and the Dog and the Ox together, and said, "Three, O Three, I'm very sorry for you (with the world so new-and-all); but that Humph-thing in the Desert can't work, or he would have been here by now, so I am going to leave him alone, and you must work double-time to make up for it."

That made the Three very angry (with the world so new-and-all), and they held a palaver, and an *indaba*, and a *punchayet*, and a pow-wow on the edge of the Desert; and the Camel came chewing milkweed *most* 'scruciating idle, and laughed at them. Then he said "Humph!" and went away again.

Presently there came along the Djinn in charge of All Deserts, rolling in a cloud of dust (Djinns always travel that way because it is Magic), and he stopped to palaver and pow-wow with the Three.

"Djinn of All Deserts," said the Horse, "*is* it right

for any one to be idle, with the world so new-and-all?"

"Certainly not," said the Djinn.

"Well," said the Horse, "there's a thing in the middle of your Howling Desert (and he's a Howler himself) with a long neck and long legs, and he hasn't done a stroke of work since Monday morning. He won't trot."

"Whew!" said the Djinn, whistling, "that's my Camel, for all the gold in Arabia! What does he say about it?"

"He says 'Humph!'" said the Dog; "and he won't fetch and carry."

"Does he say anything else?"

"Only 'Humph!'; and he won't plough," said the Ox.

"Very good," said the Djinn, "I'll humph him if you will kindly wait a minute."

The Djinn rolled himself up in his dust-cloak, and took a bearing across the desert, and found the Camel most 'scruciatingly idle, looking at his own reflection in a pool of water.

"My long and bubbling friend," said the Djinn, "what's this I hear of your doing no work, with the world so new-and-all?"

"Humph!" said the Camel.

The Djinn sat down, with his chin in his hand, and began to think a Great Magic, while the Camel looked at his own reflection in the pool of water.

"You've given the Three extra work ever since
Monday morning, all on account of your
'scruciating idleness," said the Djinn; and he went
on thinking Magics, with his chin in his hand.

"Humph!" said the Camel.

"I shouldn't say that again if I were you," said
the Djinn; "you might say it once too often.
Bubbles, I want you to work."

And the Camel said "Humph!" again; but no

sooner had he said it than he saw his back, that he was so proud of, puffing up and puffing up into a great big lolloping humph.

"Do you see that?" said the Djinn. "That's your very own humph that you've brought upon yourself by not working. To-day is Thursday, and you've done no work since Monday, when the work began. Now you are going to work."

"How can I," said the Camel, "with this humph on my back?"

"That's made a-purpose," said the Djinn, "all because you missed those three days. You will be

able to work now for three days without eating, because you can live on your humph; and don't you ever say I never did anything for you. Come out of the Desert and go to the Three, and behave. Humph yourself!"

And the Camel humphed himself, humph and all, and went away to join the Three. And from that day to this the Camel always wears a humph (we call it "hump" now, not to hurt his feelings); but he has never yet caught up with the three days that he missed at the beginning of the world, and he has never yet learned how to behave.

Acknowledgements

The publisher would like to thank the copyright holders for permission to reproduce the following copyright material:

Joan Aiken: A. M. Heath & Co. Ltd. on behalf of Joan Aiken for "Eggs" from *Never Meddle With Magic and Other Stories* chosen by Barbara Ireson, Puffin Books 1988. Copyright © Joan Aiken Enterprises Ltd. 1986. **Ruth Ainsworth**: Egmont Children's Books Ltd., London for "The Bear Who Liked Hugging People" from *The Bear Who Liked Hugging People and Other Stories* by Ruth Ainsworth, William Heinemann Ltd. 1976. Copyright © Ruth Ainsworth 1976. **Leila Berg**: "The Soup-Stone" from *Topsy Turvy Tales* by Leila Berg, Methuen Children's Books Ltd. 1984 reprinted by kind permission of Leila Berg and The Lisa Eveleigh Literary Agency. Copyright © Leila Berg 1966. **Joyce Lankester Brisley**: Kingfisher Publications Plc. for "Milly-Molly-Mandy Goes Blackberrying" from *Milly-Molly-Mandy Stories* by Joyce Lankester Brisley, George G. Harrap 1928. Copyright © Joyce Lankester Brisley 1928. **Wendy Eyton**: The author for "The Woman Who Grew Butterflies" from *Tales from the Threepenny Bit* by Wendy Eyton, William Collins Sons & Co. Ltd. 1990. Copyright © Wendy Eyton 1990. **Anne Fine**: David Higham Associates Ltd. for "Hetty" by Anne Fine from *How Big Jo Tamed the Lion and Other Stories for Four-Year-Olds* collected by Julia Eccleshare, William Collins Sons & Co. Ltd. 1991. **Pippa Goodhart**: The author for "Happy Birthday, Nana Barbara!". Copyright © Pippa Goodhart 2000. **Terry Jones**: Pavilion Books for "The Glass Cupboard" from *Fairy Tales* by Terry Jones, Pavilion Books Ltd. 1981. Copyright © Terry Jones 1981. **Dick King-Smith**: A. P. Watt Ltd. on behalf of Fox Busters Ltd. for "Zap!" from *More Animal Stories* by Dick King-Smith, Puffin Books 1999. Copyright © Dick King-Smith 1987. **Rudyard Kipling**: A. P. Watt Ltd. on behalf of The National Trust for Places of Historic Interest or Natural Beauty for "How the Camel got his Hump" from *Just So Stories* by Rudyard Kipling, Puffin Books 1987. **Julius Lester**: The Random House Group Ltd. for "Brer Rabbit to the Rescue" from *The Tales of Uncle Remus* by Julius Lester, The Bodley Head 1987. Copyright © Julius Lester 1987. **Daphne Lister**: The author for "The Thirteen Cats" from *The Chair of Dreams and Other Stories and Poems* by Daphne Lister, Hodder & Stoughton Ltd. 1984. Copyright © Daphne Lister 1984. **Gillian McClure**: Scholastic Ltd. for "What's the Time, Rory Wolf?" by Gillian McClure, André Deutsch Children's Books (an imprint of Scholastic Ltd.) 1982. **Margaret Mahy**: The Orion Publishing Group Ltd. for "The Strange Egg" from *The First Margaret Mahy Story Book* by

More Kingfisher Treasuries to enjoy:

A TREASURY OF STORIES FOR
FIVE YEAR OLDS

Meet a talkative cat, a sea-baby and a giant
who throws tantrums in this enchanting
collection of stories from around the world.
Five year olds will delight in their very own
treasure-trove of words and pictures.

*"... magical stories that are a pleasure
to read aloud and that will thrill both
reader and listener."*
– SCHOOL LIBRARIAN

A TREASURY OF STORIES FOR
SIX YEAR OLDS

A flying postman, some musical animals and
a magical porridge pot – meet them all in this
delightful collection of traditional and
contemporary tales specially selected for
six year olds.

*"... simple and direct ... informed with a
zestful humour ..."*
– T.E.S.

A TREASURY OF STORIES FOR
SEVEN YEAR OLDS

Meet a heroic hare, a ship crewed by mice,
and a woman who lives in a bottle, along with
other characters from all over the world, in
this charming collection of stories for
seven year olds.

*". . . intelligently selected . . . for dipping into
again and again . . ."*
– THE SUNDAY TIMES

A TREASURY OF STORIES FOR
EIGHT YEAR OLDS

A ticklish tiger, a wise wizard and a family
of ghastly ghosts all join in the fun in this
marvellous mix of traditional and
contemporary tales from around the world.

A fabulous story collection every
eight year old will enjoy.

A TREASURY OF BEDTIME STORIES

Every child loves a story at bedtime – and
here are twenty of the very best to choose
from. Alongside favourite characters such as
Snow White, Rumpelstiltskin and Mrs Pepperpot,
there are giants and princesses, a pipe-smoking
skunk, and a monkey with a red umbrella.

The perfect book to curl up with
at the end of the day.

A TREASURY OF FUNNY STORIES

Sixteen of the funniest stories around are
gathered together in one rib-tickling volume.
From flying dogs to dancing cows, with favourite
characters such as Posy Bates, Dilly the Dinosaur
and Anancy the Spiderman joining in the fun,
this is the book for all children who love a
good giggle!

". . . [a] lively collection . . . for families to enjoy."
– BOOKS FOR KEEPS

A TREASURY OF PIRATE STORIES

There are parrots, planks and eye patches
aplenty in this treasure chest of pirate tales.
Bold buccaneers sail the Seven Seas in search of
adventure, while pirate school pupils get up to
all sorts of comic capers. Meanwhile, famous
sea salts Captain Hook and Long John Silver
are intent on their usual skulduggery . . .

Full of swashbuckling fun, this rumbustious
collection will delight all young children.

A TREASURY OF BALLET STORIES

This sparkling collection of stories from some
of today's favourite writers will enchant any
child who loves ballet. From the excitement
of learning a few first steps to the chaos of
rehearsal and the end-of-year show, the
sheer joy of dancing shines through!

The perfect book for every young ballet fan.